Licensed exclusively to Top That Publishing Ltd
Tide Mill Way, Woodbridge, Suffolk, IP12 1AP, UK
www.topthatpublishing.com
Text and illustrations copyright © 2013 Cherie Zamazing
All rights reserved
2 4 6 8 9 7 5 3 1
Printed and bound in China

Illustrated and written by Cherie Zamazing

ISBN 978-1-78244-059-8

A catalogue record for this book is available from the British Library

Peter's Pebbles

By Cherie Zamazing

'To my mum Elaine for her ever-inspiring imagination, endless love and support and to Nanny and BooBoo for always believing in me.'

Peter loved collecting pebbles – large ones, small ones, thin ones, fat ones, round ones, flat ones! He painted his pebbles to look like all sorts of different animals.

One day, as Peter was putting
his newly-painted fish pebble on the shelf,
he slipped and the pebble SPLOSHED into his fish bowl.

Suddenly, there was a flash
of light and a BUBBLE and a FIZZ!
Peter jumped back and saw a new colourful fish swimming
around the fish bowl. Peter's pebble had come to life!

'Wow! If my fish pebble came to life in water, maybe my parrot pebble will come to life in the air!' Peter thought, excitedly.

Peter opened his window
and threw his parrot pebble out into the air!

SQUAWK!

With a **SWISH** and a **SWOOP**,
Peter's pebble came to life!

Peter then picked up his monkey pebble.
'Hmm, monkeys like bananas,' he thought.
So he put the pebble into the fruit bowl!

In an instant, the fruit EXPLODED
everywhere and then …

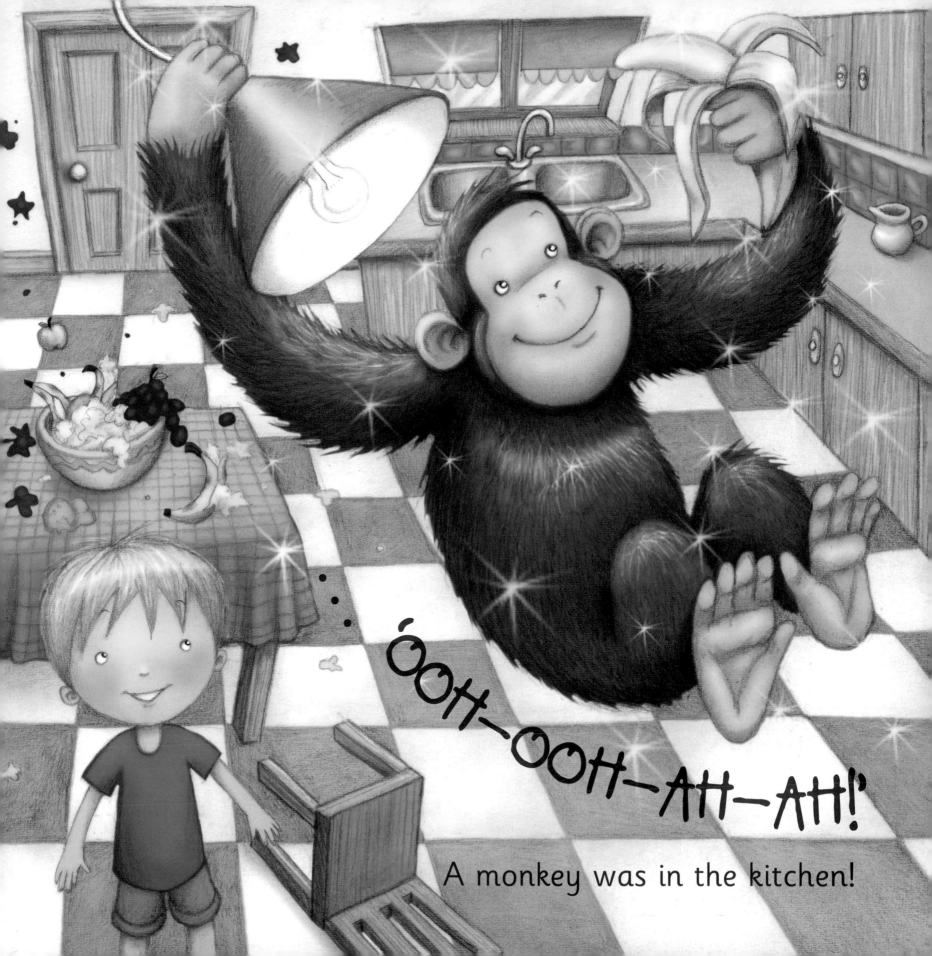

'OOH–OOH–AH–AH!'

A monkey was in the kitchen!

Next, Peter took his crocodile pebble into the bathroom. He filled the bath full of water, and dropped in the pebble. There was a BUBBLE and a SPLASH and Peter couldn't believe his eyes when a huge crocodile appeared in the bath!

Back in his bedroom, Peter showed the animals his map and pointed out where in the world they normally lived.

Just then, Peter's mum called ...

'Peter! Your dinner is ready!'

SHHHHH!

'Wait here,'
Peter said to the animals.

While Peter was downstairs, the monkey picked up the rest of Peter's painted pebbles and placed them on the map where Peter had said they lived.

Suddenly, Peter could hear an almighty commotion coming from upstairs. Luckily, Mum and Dad were too busy talking to notice. Peter quickly finished his food and raced back to his bedroom.

Peter gasped when he saw that all of his painted pebbles had come to life!

'I'll get in trouble if you stay here. I need to find a place for you all to live!'

Then, Peter had an idea!

He ran to his cupboard and pulled out a huge pebble.
He had been saving it, but he hadn't known what to
paint until now ...

Peter waited
until everyone
was asleep and then
led the animals quietly
out of the house and down
to the beach.

Peter climbed into his boat, and together he and the animals swam, rowed and flew out into the ocean.

When they had travelled
far enough, Peter lifted the
big pebble into the air and
threw it with all his might!

Immediately, there was a deep rumbling sound and the boat began to rock as the waves rose higher and higher …

Suddenly, out of the waves a huge island appeared!
There were jungles full of plants and palm trees,
clear blue streams, waterfalls, mountains
and, of course, a yellow sandy beach,
just as Peter had painted
on his large pebble!

As the sun came up, all of the happy animals waved goodbye to Peter as he rowed his way back home!

'I'll visit you soon!' he called.

As Peter reached the shore,
he spotted a very strange-shaped pebble.
'Hmm, I wonder what I can paint next,' he thought.

More great picture books from Top That Publishing

ISBN 978-1-78244-064-2

A rhyming storybook, full of nonsense, by inimitable author, Edward Lear.

ISBN 978-1-78244-073-4

This tale, full of fun and folly, recalls the Quangle Wangle and his delightful hat.

ISBN 978-1-84956-778-7

A fantastical tale about a boy and the adventures he has with his rocking horse.

ISBN 978-1-78244-040-6

Follow the little raindrop's adventure and learn all about the water cycle.

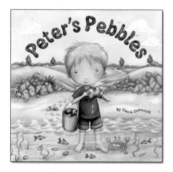

ISBN 978-1-78244-059-8

Peter's pebbles come to life in this perfectly crafted tale, full of imagination.

ISBN 978-1-78244-074-1

Cammy the colourful chameleon learns an important lesson in this vibrant tale.

ISBN 978-1-78244-170-0

Something mysterious is following poor kitty. Whatever can it be?

ISBN 978-1-78244-189-2

An enchanting tale about an elusive mouse that nobody notices ... do you?

ISBN 978-1-78244-109-0

Search the beautifully illustrated tale to find the hidden ghosts.

ISBN 978-1-78244-187-8

A heartwarming tale about the magic of children's love and creativity.

ISBN 978-1-84956-438-0

A fantastical tale about unruly morning hair and a mischievous fairy.

ISBN 978-1-84956-439-7

The animal food chain is turned upside-down in this funny story with a twist.

Available from all good bookstores or visit www.topthatpublishing.com
Look for Top That Apps in the Apple iTunes Store